Forty-one Leaves

Eleven Pauses

Israr

Contents

Coffee and Cigarettes   1

Less and Far   21

Empty Space   27

Life, Father and Son   33

Ramblings   41

A Meeting with Fireflies   45

If Pain is the Only Way   61

You Are the Moon and I the Sea   65

A Traveller (Wind and Tree)   69

Sparkling Eyes   81

Captain and Minion   85

Coffee and Cigarettes

Leon is a 42 year old special task force captain. His is a strong body that carries an even stronger mind. He respects subordinates, smiles often, and opens his heart to everyone. Luckily, he doesn't cross the thin line between courage and stupidity (most of the time).

Asad is a 37 year old man. Strict on rules. Crosses his "T"s and dots his "I"s. Nevertheless, he has a pure heart. He would forgive someone for breaking the law, but never himself.

Asad and Leon have known each other for 12 years. They are equals, but Asad respects Leon like an older brother. Leon never asked why nor took advantage of it.

In the country where Leon and Asad reside, the army is very powerful, and army officials can very much do as they please, provided no one dies. Asad was told an hour ago to report to a high security detention center that also serves as an execution ground. A death row inmate has requested Asad to carry out his execution. The request is being honoured. The inmate to be executed: Captain Leon.

Asad keeps his composure. The building he enters is only two stories high, but fenced with half a mile of grass all around. Asad heads to Leon's cell which is being personally guarded by a soldier.

Sergeant: It is very dangerous to approach the prisoner, please do not enter the cell.

Asad merely glares at the soldier and holds his hand out. He barely manages to remain civil as he takes the key and opens the cell.

Leon sees Asad coming and straightens up in his chair. He has a black eye that's almost not open, dried blood in his hair, and a couple of broken ribs.

Asad opens the door to the cell. And upon seeing his friend's state he loses it. And shouts...

Asad: Who did this to Captain Leon? Who was in charge of the arrest and transport?

Asad whirls on the soldier guarding the cell. The blood drains from the guard's face as he stands up.

Leon: Whoa! Asad calm down. Could you get me a glass of water?

Asad barely hears this, but goes back to the cell.

Asad: You okay, Cap?

Leon: Yeah I'm fine. Those guys punch like elitists. (Smiles in a peculiar way, something he always does.) Do you mind uncuffing me? And I am parched, mate.

Asad: (Unlocks the cell, goes inside and uncuffs Leon) Who did this to you? What happened? (Avoids the question he cannot bring himself to ask.)

Leon: (Sighs in relief) glass of water and a pack of fags, mate. And, uh, I want coffee from that fancy place. (Big smile.)

Asad: (Doesn't move and looks at his friend in desperation) What happened?

Leon: (Reads the desperation in his friend's eyes and decides to tell him. He speaks a little robotically) I killed the pig. And got arrested.

Asad: (Rubs his forehead in frustration) And the clowns in here did this to you, didn't they?

Leon: (Looks at his friend and with a very grave face) The young men who work here are full of energy and—

Asad: So you just stood there and took it?

Leon: He probably has a family.

Asad: (Hears the request in friend's tone: please, don't punish him. Takes a deep breath. Starts looking like a bewildered animal ready to attack.)

Leon: (Knows his friend is in a rough spot) Asad... it's going to be a long night, sit down.

Asad: (Still shaken) I'll get you that coffee.

Leon: (Adds with a slightly humorous voice) A pack of fags and water too.

Asad: (Looks over his shoulder slightly and nods. Asad approaches the guard, a sergeant) Bring me a pack of cigarettes, bottle of water, and one coffee... make that two coffees.

Sergeant: Sir, are you sure? He's a rogue.

Asad: (Half-turned away already but stops. He notices the sergeant's bloody shoes and bruised hand.) You made the arrest, didn't you?

Sergeant: (Defensively) Yes, Sir.

Asad: That man in the cell spared your life thinking of your family. And he saved it again by holding me back. Because, by God! If he hadn't you would have been eating your food through a straw. Do you honestly think you arrested him? He's here because he wanted to be here. Did he resist arrest?

Sergeant: No, Sir.

Asad: Then why would you... (Somberly) Start walking before you learn what a man half Captain Leon's caliber can do to you.

Sergeant: (Does not make eye contact) Yes, Sir. (And walks away quickly.)

Asad: Stop! Do you have cigarettes on you?

Asad returns to the cell with a cup of house-coffee, bottle of water, and half a pack of cigarettes.

Leon: (Is sitting completely expressionless, hard to read as always.)

Asad: (Loosens up, sits across from Leon.) What happened, man? (Places the coffee and water next to Leon and hands him the pack with the lighter inside it.)

Leon: He was rotten. Everyone knew it and—

Asad: So, you just go up to him and kill him?

Leon: More or less, yes.

Asad: Leon, you have to give me more than this.

Leon: (Hears the plea in his friend's voice.) People complain, protest, hurt each other, and what not. I don't do that. I don't see the point in that... either you bear the pain or fix it. Crying about it doesn't help. The bugger wore diamond studded watches! Can you imagine how much—where did he get the money from? (Shakes head and composes himself.) Have you seen those little kids at traffic lights cleaning the car windscreens? Have you seen how desperate ... all that money—just from one car—could change so much... how could I not have killed him? Isn't that the right question?

The Sergeant returns, interrupting them. Leon and Asad are interrupted by the approach of an officer.

Sergeant: Sir, the doctor is here.

Asad is asked to leave for privacy. Asad and Leon both nod to each other. The doctor, who sits outside his closed cell door, in plain clothes, grey hair, and a steady pace, exudes normalcy to the extent that it stands out. His faint smile is barely there, looking as small as possible.

Doctor: Captain Leon, my name is Tenebris Hora. I am a doctor and here to speak with you.

Leon smiles half mocking and half acknowledging, maybe even admiring.

Leon: (Drinks from the water bottle.) Doctor! How may I be of service?

Doctor: You could answer my questions to the best of your knowledge. (The doctor exudes a docile attitude.)

Leon: (Smiles again, fainter this time.)

Doctor: So, Leon—may I call you Leon?

Leon: No.

Doctor: (Doesn't react and corrects himself.) Captain Leon, how are you feeling?

Leon: I am feeling well, Doctor. (Sips his coffee and lights a cigarette.) Coffee, a cigarette, and (looks around) a warm cell. What more can a man ask for?

Doctor: (Holds his breath for a little bit, points towards Leon's face and the blood on his shirt.) Doesn't it bother you?

Leon: (Laughs heartily.) Not really, Doctor (with a faint smile and a gaze that would melt a rock). All in a good day's work.

Doctor: (Starts to scribble for the first time.) Captain Leon, do you think it was good of you to kill Mayor Hermes?

Leon: It's never good to kill anyone. Sadly, a lot of good can come from killing some people.

Doctor: Good to whom?

Leon: People... society.

Doctor: Do you think you're a savior?

Leon: (A bit loudly, with his eyes fixed on the doctor) Doctor! Why don't *you* tell me what to say, and I'll say that. Then we could both call it a night!

Doctor: (Feigns a little surprise) I am merely asking questions.

Leon: (Monotone) Then stop manipulating me... word feeding me. I am not very smart, but I am not *that* dumb. You walk in here, introduce yourself without a suffix, try to call me by my first name ...you are good, but you're not my friend, Doctor, and you certainly do not know me. So, please, stop acting like you do. You want to talk, then talk. Otherwise, bugger off. I don't have a lot of time to waste.

Doctor: (Nods as if in agreement, and puts his pen back into his pocket.) You are going to die tomorrow, yet you say you are fine. Does it not affect you in any way?

The doctor's tone changes, which Leon picks up.

Leon: (Takes a hearty drag.) It bothers me. But crying is just so tedious. (Cracks a little smile.)

The doctor's expression seems to have softened a little. He recognizes the fear in Leon's voice and the courage that conceals it.

Doctor: And killing a man, how does that feel?

Leon: (Shrugs.) I have killed for this country before. It bothered me a lot, and I lost sleep. Then I learned how to live with it.

Doctor: But this was an innocent man.

Leon: (Grimaces.) Come on, Doctor. He wasn't. He was just too powerful to get caught, and you know it. (Takes a deep drag and exhales audibly.)

Doctor: (Thinks. The façade cracks ever so slightly.)

Leon throws his pack of cigarettes and lighter towards the doctor.

Doctor: What gave me away? I didn't even look.

Leon: Exactly.

Doctor: (Smiles faintly, and lights a cigarette.) Did you hate him so much that you threw away your own life?

Leon: I never considered my life to be worth a lot. If it were up to me I would have never existed. (Continues talking as if answering the doctor's question). Do you miss your talking dog? (Doctor looks at Leon skeptically.) How can you miss someone or something that doesn't exist? How could I have treasured or missed this life? And my loved ones would have been fine too. With that understood there is no point in dwelling over something so trivial.

Doctor: Is life not a gift?

Leon: Not to me. I am grateful for what I have but I would rather not be than be.

Doctor: So, what was the point of it all?

Leon: A man killed himself in protest and a revolution started. Many before him have killed themselves in protest, and nothing happened. I don't think my death will bring much. I dare say, I have the courage to do wrong. So I did it.

Doctor: What do you mean "the courage to do wrong"?

Leon: I did what I did. Was it wrong in the eyes of the law? Yes. Do I think it was the right thing to do? Yes. Do I expect to be forgiven? No. Would I do it again? Yes. Do I have the honour to admit it? Yes.

(Realizes he is speaking loudly and mellows a little.) In short, hang me or rank me, it's not my decision, nor does it matter.

Doctor: (Smokes quietly.) I have been doing this for some time now. Rarely have I seen honour and integrity. It's a sad day, Captain Leon ... from what I have concluded, you rid society of an evil and you were in your senses when you did it?

Leon: (Nods.)

Doctor: (To Leon's surprise, walks over to the cell to hand back the lighter and the pack of cigarettes. He reads the surprise on Leon's face.) Captain, I do this for a living. I know you won't kill me.

Leon stands up and takes it, at which point the doctor offers his hand to shake. Leon accepts.

Doctor: Why not report him to authorities?

Leon: I didn't have proof. This was the easiest way. What's one man's life worth when you're saving millions?

Doctor: I believe I understand. I beg your leave, Captain.

Now alone in the cell, twenty minutes stretch on longer than they deserve. Eventually, Asad returns with two cups and a brown bag.

Leon: Where have you been?

Asad: The Doctor had some questions and I thought I would get you something to eat. A latte with four sugars and a cinnamon roll.

Leon: Victory!! (Devours the roll and sips the hot latte gingerly.) This is really good. Not the best coffee, but the roll is really good.

Asad: (Nods while sitting across from Leon. Asad reaches for the pack of cigarettes and lights one.)

Leon: (Leon understands the difficult situation his friend is going through. Tries to lift the mood) Do you think they'll have this where I am going?

Asad: (Still deep in thought shrugs.)

Leon: Asad, you should know that I am really sorry.

Asad: (Frowns) What about?

Leon: For getting you into a situation like this. It was unintentional, but still I am sorry.

Asad: Shut up and worry about yourself you buffoon.

Leon: You will do it, right? I want you to.

Asad: (Silent.)

Leon: I would rather be sitting next to you, a brave man and a true friend, than someone I don't know. You'd do it, right? For me?

Asad: (Greatly disturbed, nods.)

Leon: Sorry, I am making this about my--

Asad: (Shouts) --Would you shut up! Just shut up.

Leon: (Eats quietly. Then he points at Asad's watch.)

Asad: Prayer?

Leon: Yes.

Asad: (Nods)

Leon goes to the corner of the cell and starts to pray.

Asad has seen Leon pray many times - standing, quiet and humble. Leon takes his time. He sits cross-legged. Somehow watching Leon soothes Asad. Makes Asad feel like everything will be fine. When he stands, his eyes are moist.

Asad: (A regular question that he never failed to ask.) What did you ask for?

Leon: Forgiveness. Strength to bear what comes my way, and guidance for you. (This last bit always made them both smile just like tonight.)

At this point they hear voices, accompanied by footsteps. Leon is surprised. Asad is not. Leon notices his friend not reacting.

Five men enter the corridor followed by soldiers. Five chairs are set in front of the cell.

Leon: (Looks at Asad) You did this. Didn't you?

Asad: (With pleading eyes looks at Leon) Please, Leon. We have a chance. Please. Try. For me.

Leon: (Wants to say he will say how things are, but relents to Asads plea and nods.)

Leon notices the shrink from earlier is one of the five.

Shrink: (In a loud authoritative voice.) Leon, Captain Leon. We are here upon Major Asad's request and my discretion. This is an unusual case, and we have decided to give you a chance to have your say. Captain Leon, you are being tried for the murder of Mayor Hermes. We shall hear your side of the story, and it is solely up to our discretion to see where this goes. Bear in mind, four votes are needed to overturn your pending sentence. Do you understand?

Leon: Yes, Sir.

Shrink: Do you wish to continue?

Leon: (Almost laughs and wants to say "do I have a choice?") Yes, Sir.

Shrink: Gentlemen.

Leon stands straight and looks ahead at nothing, as does every other soldier present.

4th chair: You were caught red handed, do you deny killing Mayor Hermes?

Leon: No, Sir. I killed Mayor Hermes.

1st chair: It says you shot him once in the chest and once in the head. You were well in control of yourself and aware of what you were doing, were you not?

Leon: I was.

1st chair: We rule out momentary madness.

Shrink: You are a trained soldier. Perhaps that's why you did not hesitate. Was there any personal animosity, or were you pressured by anyone in any way?

Leon: No, sir. I planned and executed it by myself.

3rd chair: Why did you kill Mayor Hermes, son?

Leon: He was a corrupt leader. He didn't care for the people. He robbed them of their rights. His mansions and luxuries could have fed and educated many. He had to be stopped. No one had the nerve. Those who did were either silenced or lost their lives. He wasn't going away.

2nd chair: (Each word cold and deliberate) So, you decided to play "hero of the day"?

Asad feels Leon's body tense.

2nd chair: Tell me, Captain, what did you expect would happen? Did you think you would have been honoured as a hero? Maybe a monument to commemorate your courage?

Leon: (Made eye contact with the person sitting in the 2nd chair and noticed the expensive watch and ring. Even though he was not wearing a uniform. He had the air of someone who thought he was superior to everyone else.) No, Sir. I was well aware of the consequences. With all due respect, you do not have capable enough men to capture me alive. I accept what I did.

2nd chair: (Smiles arrogantly.) So, you don't regret it?

Leon: The only way some good could have been achieved was by taking one man's life. Someone had to get their hands dirty. I don't regret it.

3rd chair: So, you would kill anyone who is corrupt?

Leon: Anyone just as corrupt as he and whose death may help others.

Silence.

Shrink: Are there any other questions?

Shrink: Then we shall now reach a verdict.

They sat and spoke to each other in whispers. Some shook their heads and some nodded. After what seemed like an eternity to Asad, the doctor spoke.

Shrink: All those in favour of the pending sentence, raise your hands.

All but the Doctor and the 3rd chair raise their hands.

Shrink: That's one more than what is needed to see the sentence through. Thank you for your time gentlemen.

Asad: Permission to speak, sir.

Shrink: (Ignores the glares from the others.) Speak, soldier. Make it short.

Asad: I shall be Captain Leon's guarantor. Please, reconsider.

Shrink: (Looks at the seated men, who seem like they don't want to be kept any longer.) Quick vote gentlemen. Those in favour of releasing Captain Leon and setting Major Asad as his guarantor raise your hands.

The 1st chair adds his hand to the Doctor and the 3rd chair.

Shrink: Denied. You have till 0800 hours. Once again, thank you for your time gentlemen.

The seated men, except for the doctor, leave.

Shrink: (Walks up to Leon. His tone mild.) You did this country a favour, son. I am sorry I couldn't do anything for you. If there is anything you want...

Leon: A shower, clean clothes, Major Asad to sit next to me, and a proper funeral.

Shrink: Done.

Leon: ...Exactly who are you?

Shrink: (Smirks. It was hard to believe it was the same shrink who spoke to Leon not too long ago.) It's above your pay grade soldier. (Points to the cigarette pack. Leon hands him one and lights it for him.) Damn shame. But just too many people want you dead. (Walks away without another word.)

Asad: (Disheartened.)

Leon: (Turns to Asad, who now sits slumped inside the cell.) Chin up, solder! Pull yourself together.

Asad: (Sounds confused and almost talking to himself) I don't know what to do. I want to let you go. I want you to live. I... can get you out.

Leon: You're a soldier! (Speaks in a slow steady voice. Leon recites a war chant) We are men. We live by our words and actions. We are brothers in arms. May my strike be just. May the bullets pierce me before my brother. May my hands not harm the weak. May God give us strength to face foe, storms, or death with dignity.

By the end there was a small chorus that had been taken up by the guards down the hall. Even Asad joined in a low voice. A soldier approaches the cell and salutes.

Soldier: I have been ordered to provide you with fresh clothes. Would you like me to go to your house and get you some?

Leon: Asad, you got anything I could borrow? My house is locked and, honest, I don't know where the key is.

Asad: Yes. (He instructs the soldier to go to his house.)

Meanwhile Leon and Asad sit quietly, and this time Asad breaks the ice.

Asad: You okay?

Leon: (Smiles. Unreadable as ever) Yes.

Asad: (Doesn't know what to say.)

Leon: It's not that big a deal. You think this and that. Whenever I heard of people on their death beds, I imagined they had a lot to say. I imagined I would have a lot to say. But now that the time is nigh. (Shrugs.) It's time to face what I did in my life. People say big words like legacy, values, name, and what not. It doesn't matter, not when you're dead. A good deed will prevail, good teachings, but why all the drama. Do what you have to and be done with it. A lot of good people die unfair deaths. I am neither good nor will my death be unfair. I digress. (Smiles) Death is death. It's like fearing an exam. When the time finally comes you are calm. The bell has rung, and I have stopped writing. Know what I mean?

Asad: Yes. I think so.

Leon: And according your views I'm going to back to nature. Nothing to it. (Shakes his head) Let's laugh, my friend. I don't like drama. You know that.

Asad: Haah. Says the drama queen.

They speak for a while. Some loud laughter and another pack of cigarettes later the soldier arrives with the fresh change of clothes. They arrange for Leon to take a shower. He cleans up, dresses, and breathes freely.

Leon: Let's go.

They both walk to the execution room. Leon is left unrestrained. He sits cross legged, and has Major Asad sit next to him. He wraps his arm around Major Asad in a short half-embrace.

The doctor is present. He wipes the inside of Leon's right arm with an alcoholic swab. As he pricks Leon's skin Leon winces.

Leon: Always hated these bloody needles.

Leon looks to all those present in the room.

Leon: Peace be upon you.

Soon his body relaxes a little and then goes limp, leaning against Major Asad. No one moves. Asad sits next to his dead friend in silence.

The funeral was very small. Asad helped with the burial. No one called Leon a hero. No monuments were erected. No stories of his bravery were ever shared. He was only missed by his friend. Only Asad remembered him, but he knew, for Leon, that was more than enough.

Less and Far

Less-than-far Wise and Far-than-less Wise are two friends. They haven't known each other for very long, but in a short while they have become closer than they once were. They meet at their, currently, favourite restaurant.

Far-than-less Wise (Far): How are you?

Less-than-far Wise (Less): I'm very well. You, how's life treating you?

Far: I'm good. Slow day, but I'm doing well.

Far is wearing a radiant smile.

Less smiles. Far notices but doesn't say anything. Less voluntarily starts talking without explaining, wanting Far to ask. Far doesn't question Less' countenance and chooses to listen.

Less: I am smiling because you're good.

Knowing Less means a lot more than just that, Far doesn't play along. Far shows no sign of curiosity and suggests it in a way that merely shows Far is humoring Less. All the while smiling in the same fashion.

Less is uncertain of how Far feels but continues regardless.

Less: You have a strong defense: your expressions don't give you away. You reveal only what you choose to.

Far squints slightly and looks at Less closely, evaluating the statement.

Far: Does it bother you?

Less: Not at all. It's admirable. However, I can't help but feel ... that it might be lonely?

Less continues pausing long enough to raise the question if Less is wrong. Less picks up the subtle changes in the atmosphere that almost aren't there. Without making eye contact but always watching, as second-nature. Part hoping Far knows of this since otherwise it would be unethical.

Less: Not expressing much is a tad tiring. Also, one is easily misjudged. (Quickly adding) not that it should matter. Just that it's usually lonely on top of the hill.

Far: I do express myself.

Less continues in a modest tone not sure how far Less can push. Choosing words carefully, Less lays them out.

Less: Yes, yes you do, just not your emotions. Which makes it harder for me.

Far gives another quizzical look. Humoring what Less has to say. But this time Far is genuinely curious.

Less smiles and lets the reason for it linger in Far's mind in the form of a question.

Less: I don't know what to do. I care for you. And not knowing how you feel makes it hard for me at times. I don't want to judge you. But... you know...

Far is touched. Less can't tell if Far is offended. Since it could backfire into something like "no one asked you to care for me" or "if it's tiring don't do it". But Far, being shrewd and subtle, simply speaks with the same smile and aura.

Far: I'm happy. You don't have to be worry for me.

Less tries to be as honest as possible, with a serious tone, so that Far may understand what Less finds difficult to express.

Less: It's not that—I do not question your happiness. It's just, I wonder if you would actually tell me if you *weren't* happy. If you *should* tell me? Is it my place to ask? Shouldn't I, as your friend, be able to tell? I feel guilty. And ... I wonder if I actually have the right to say all that I just did?

Far continues to smile as before. Less ponders, trying to analyze the damage.

Waiter comes to take their order. The atmosphere changes, and they begin to order.

After the waiter has left and the dust in their minds settled. This time, Less knows exactly what to say, and the inevitable happens. Less continues to explain, but, this time, sure to hit the nail on the head.

Less: Often what is guarded dearly is extremely delicate. Often the guarded are in solitude.

Far is amused to the point of laughing out loud. The sheer joy of it. Far wonders what a person like Less is doing in this era. Why Less has to go to such extremes, and if it is all genuine. Far decides not to play anymore. Far smiles.

Far: I am fine, thank you for caring.

Less doesn't respond just looks back. With a faint genuine smile Less chooses to settle for what is being given.

The food arrives. Once again everything changes to nothing really that has to do with anything. Laughter and jokes follow.

Empty Space

Asrar: Hey, just in time.

Talal: Yo was'up was'up? In time for what?

Asrar: I'm making some coffee. (Opens a jar, looks inside and gives it a little shake.) And I've exactly got enough for two cups. Care for one?

Talal: Please.

Asrar: (Puts the kettle on)

Talal: So, bro. How you doing?

Asrar: Good. Aching here and there. I'm getting old.

Talal: You know that joke is getting old, right?

Asrar: (Smiles) So what's up with you? You look like you've had it rough.

Talal: One of those days, man. You know.

Asrar furrows his eye brows. Talal gets the message.

Talal: Last night I spoke to a friend after a long time. It was good catching up but it was as if we were different people. So, before going to bed I just started thinking about things, the past, this and that. I fell asleep with mixed feelings and woke up feeling … Almost nothing. I don't know what to feel man. You know. It's just … (Talal looks away to look for words that would justify his thoughts. Unsure he continues.) I don't know man. The way people change and the way things happen. How you're strangers then acquaintances then friends and then back to strangers. It makes me think of a lot of things but at the same time nothing in particular. I guess I just feel empty. So yeah … (Talal pauses … to evaluate what he is saying. Wonders if Asrar understands. If Talal himself understands) … Anyway, how was your game last night?

Asrar tends to the kettle. He adds sugar and dismisses the topic of his game by saying "you win some…" followed by a shrug. He hands Talal a cup of coffee.

Asrar: So, you feel empty?

Talal: I guess so. I mean, I feel nothing, is that even possible? You know what I mean right?

Asrar: Being unsure of what one feels, open to all sorts of interpretation?

Talal: I guess so.

Asrar ponders for a moment or two, then reaches for the empty coffee jar.

Asrar: Your feelings are like this jar right now. Empty indeed; however, still occupying space. Mate, it doesn't matter what's inside it. What matters is "what" you fill it with.

Talal: (Processing) Okay.

Asrar: Voids have to be filled. We, as humans, tend to fill voids with thoughts the make us feel empty and in essence disconnected. Don't do that. Choose to be happy or don't let it affect you. Until you find out what you want to fill up the jar with. Make sense?

Talal: (Thinking) It does, bro. it does.

Empty Space

Asrar sips his coffee, giving Talal the space to think.

Asrar: Enough of Doctor Phil repeats. What we doing today?

Life, Father and Son

Father is a man of 52 full of life.

Son is a 17 year old young man. Very smart and mature for his age.

Father senses his son has something on his mind. Father does not tell his wife for she will worry much. Besides, since he doesn't know what his son is going through, a sit down may be too much. He decides to go for a walk in the park with his son.

Father: So, how has school been?

Son: Good.

Father: And your friends?

Son: Good.

Father: You seem a little upset. (Starts with a firm tone, but ends in a very gentle way.)

Son: I'm not upset.

Father: What's wrong then?

Son: (Takes more than a moment) I ... I'm not sure.

Father: Hm... You know, when you were younger you would ask me plenty of questions. You even asked me once if you could marry our neighbor's daughter, and you were only five then.

Son: Well, (shy smile) *that's* really embarrassing.

Father: (Warm brief laugh) No, it's not. You asked a brave question.

Son: (Smiles shyly.)

Father: (Holds the back of his son's head and shakes him firmly.) So, what's bothering you?

Son: (Enjoys the fact that he is with his father, and can rely on him, and decides to open up.) I'm not sure. Just too many thoughts. So much is happening. It's just overwhelming. (Voice trails off.)

Father: Like?

Son: School's about to finish. Some of the kids at my school are going abroad to study. They seem really happy about it. Others are staying back. They figure they'll go to school here, or start working and pursue their dreams. But I... (struggles with thoughts).

Father: (Helps his son find words) Do you want to go abroad for higher education?

Son: No, that's not it.

Father: (A little scared, but reveals nothing.) Do you want to do something other than pursue education?

Son: That's just it! I'm not sure *what* I want. It's like everything has changed.

Father: (Genuinely curious) Like what?

Son: To me, life is family and friends. And now, everyone is leaving. Everything will change. It's all just changing so fast. I don't know what life is supposed to mean. It's like it's changed so fast, and I am not sure what it's supposed to mean. It's a bit too much, you know?

Father: (A little happy at how his son is growing up and at the same time worried for him.) Hmm. (Pauses to think) So you think life has changed?

Son: Yes.

Father: What if I said it hasn't changed. You never knew what it was.

Son: How do you mean?

Father: You didn't know what it was and will only know when you figure it out.

Son: (A little impatient) I have *no* idea what you're talking about.

Father: (Intentionally stops at a food stand to get a drink to break the flow of the conversation.) Let's get some tea first, eh? Fancy a cupper?

Son: (Disappointed, shakes head.)

Father: (Holds the cup of tea and starts to walk towards a bench.) Look at that cloud. Tell me, what do you see? (Sits next to his son and points with his head at a generally secluded round-shaped cloud.)

Son: (Surprised by the question but looks at the cloud regardless and answers unenthusiastically) A turtle.

Father: (Immediately responds while tasting from the stirrer for sugar) Wrong. Look again.

Son: I don't know!

Father: (Smiles and looks at his son) Have faith in your old man.

Look again.

Son: An elephant?

Father: (Faces his son, holds the cup in one hand. There is nothing between him and his son.) Son, that's life.

Son: (Right away is alert and starts listening intently with a perplexed look on his face.)

Father: (Without waiting for his son to say anything continues.) I see a football. Who's to say if either one of us is wrong? Life is what you make of it.

Son: What *do* I make of it, then?

Father: That's for you to decide. (Adding voluntarily) To me, life is my family. Your grandparents, uncles, and aunt. I love my friends, but it's not only about them. They come and go. If the day comes I'll stand up for them, provided I do not harm my life. I do not disappoint those who believe in me. (Pauses to think.)

Father: We have aims in life, we have dreams, and they keep changing. I wanted to pursue a good education. Then I wanted a good job, then a good wife. I wanted to be a father, then to give a good education to my children, and so on. And while doing this I wanted to keep my loved ones happy. Even sacrificed a few dreams at times. As long as I pray on time, have my loved ones with me, have a steady job to feed you lot, and the occasional sports session, I am happy, and life is beautiful. (Waits for his son to understand.)

Son: Then why did you say I was wrong when I said it was a turtle?

Father: I was hoping you would ask me that. *One*—you are still wrong. I think it's a football. (Son waiting for it to make sense). You will have plenty of disagreements in your life. Including disagreements about what life is. *Two* (smacks his son on the back of the head in good spirit. Son startles, sees his father smiling, and smiles along). You buffoon it's a cloud! Who cares what it looks like? Enjoy the view. And that's life for you. If you sit around, arguing and thinking about what it looks like, you'll look like the imbecile who's not enjoying the view. It's a cloud. We only made animals out of them when you were a child for fun. (Smiles.)

Son: (Feels his father's hand squeeze lightly. Laughs.)

Father: (Rubs the back of his sons head.) Let's head back. I wonder what your mum cooked. The other day she made this weird chicken that she saw on telly. It was horrible! (Squints and shakes his head.)

Son: I liked it.

Father: Maybe I should cook.

Son: (Just laughs.)

Son: Dad...

Father: (Responds with a grunt.)

Son: What if it doesn't work out?

Father: At times it doesn't. Keep reminding yourself of what you believe in. Do what you can, and learn to be happy. If you explore life, you'll find other people have said the same. Just don't chase too much trying to find an answer that fits perfectly. And I'm here if you need me. We can talk again.

Son: (Thinks and feels satisfied.)

They reach home.

Mother: (A little skeptically) How was your "walk in the park"?

Son: Dad said the chicken you cooked the other day was horrible.

Mother: (Looks at her husband without a word.)

Ramblings

wait... didn't i just pass this doorway not long ago?

this alley looks familiar—it leads to tomorrow

ahh tomorrow you're hard to get a hold of

i am pondering again

pondering is a luxury i cannot afford

i shouldn't stay here long, for tomorrow may just become today

and today has been long enough to last another day

there... that alleyway,

i don't remember a stream—, no one mentioned a stream

"excuse me, kind sir, could—".... "oh no i just need directions"

"yes i do work hard, i am merely lost. thank you anyway"

"i hate to be rude, but i have destiny to look for"

how did i end up here?

i was happy once; wait ... was i? i am sure i was

i know what happiness is, i—

dear oh dear, can't waste time, can't ponder ...

the sun is down, i'll just lie here and rest

oh these beautiful stars, i am sure they remind me of something ...

happiness ... they remind me of happiness, i am sure of it

"i am sorry i didn't realise the sun was up"

"thank you for waking me up"

"i am looking for destiny, would you, perhaps, like to join me?"

"i can't promise much, but if i find tomorrow i'll share it with you"

"you're happiness... aren't you? ... i dream of you, quiet often"

"why are you leaving?"

oh the stream!

i have finally found it, i can bear the hardships of it

i'll push myself ... curse these weak arms and legs

i won't give up... is this it?

this town ... i did what i was told ... is this it?

i did what ... this alley looks familiar ...

A Meeting with Fireflies

Traveler: a 17-year-old young man who thinks too much. He is taking the bus to a fair in a nearby village with his friends.

Addict: is an innocuous looking man. He is in a dismal state, carrying a couple of carry-bags in his hands and a backpack.

Traveler is waiting for the bus at a small teahouse where he sees Addict. Addict is clearly not doing too well in life. Traveler wonders what causes people to go down that road – addiction. He decides to not judge and speaks to Addict. Traveler barely gets past pleasantries, and the bus arrives. They get on the bus. Addict is sitting at the back of the bus by himself. Traveler doesn't want other people eavesdropping, and shies away from the idea of talking to Addict.

Looking out the window Addict has a strange aura about him. Half dreaming, half awake, seeing things only his eyes can see. His eyes lose their light showing despair and then suddenly he smiles like a child almost blushing to himself. He seems natural yet out of place, like he doesn't belong.

Bus stops, Addict gets off the bus, takes a few steps, and takes off his backpack. Traveler realizes that Addict will be at the bus stop for a little bit. After a quick word with his friend, Traveler gets off as well. Addict is fishing for something in his carry-bag. Addict pretends he hasn't seen Traveler and is engrossed with what's at hand.

Traveler: Hello.

No response.

Traveler: Hello. You doing alright?

No response.

Traveler feels like he is imposing. Sighs and looks around. While Addict lights up something to smoke.

Addict: (Takes a long pull and exhales loudly and thoughtfully. This catches Traveler's attention, but he quickly looks away. Addict chuckles as if laughing at his own joke making Traveler feels embarrassed even though he doesn't know why. Addict speaks with a deep dreamy voice) It's nice and warm for this time of the year, no?

Traveler: (Surprised and happy for Addict to have spoken, quickly recovers and says) Uh, yes.

Addict: (Smiles in a peculiar fashion.) You will forgive me for not responding earlier. At times I am not sure if the conversation is taking place in my head or in reality. Ergo, I choose not to respond. Scares away people otherwise. Bad for business and all that.

Traveler: (Unsure how to respond says) Um, no harm done. (Smiles nervously to show good faith. A part of him feels like the Addict is truly enjoying this, as if a mean joke.)

Addict: So?

Traveler: Uhh. I was just saying that you not responding didn't cause any harm.

Addict: (Suddenly smiles dotingly, like a parent who is trying to pacify a child who is scared.) I understood that part. *I* wanted to know what is it that *you* wanted to talk about.

Traveler: (Too slow to respond as he is trying to grasp the transition in the old man's demeanor.)

Addict: (With an equal placating tone of voice) You greeted me earlier, surely you wanted to say something. And this probably isn't even where you wanted to get off the bus. Unless you wanted to meet with the fireflies. (He waves towards the flickering lights down in the valley.)

Traveler: (Smiles for the first time.) Yes, yes. I did, and this isn't my destination either.

Addict: On with it, boy! (Traveler almost flinches. Just then Addict goes into a fit of laughter that ends in a coughing fit. He looks away and spits. When he turns around, he is slightly wheezy and out of breath. He waggles his eyebrows as if saying "yes?")

Traveler: (Is wide eyed. And starts to speak with caution) I just wanted to have a conversation. (Pauses for a response. Addict still wheezing, raises eyebrows and nods.) (Traveler starts talking again) I-

Addict: (With a stern voice) Be honest.

Traveler: (Continues) I enjoy learning very much. Seeing you I wanted to know what could have led you to using drugs. I thought the things you may tell me would be something I wouldn't be able to read or hear anywhere else.

Addict: Next bus is in about an hour and thirty minutes. Let's sit over there. (Points to a bench that faces the village below. The sun is almost down, and the lights from the village fair look beautiful from where they sit. Addict adds in a flat tone) Sure, a conversation should be nice. I have been alone for a long time and lonely for even longer.

Traveler: And you started using because of that? (Traveler is a tad skeptical.)

Addict: (In a trance and with a great calm that made Traveler shiver. Addict spoke more to himself than Traveler) Everybody wants to save the dying and no one wants to save those who are still alive. Young man, when was the last time you spoke to anyone for longer than three minutes?

Traveler: (Perplexed by the question) I spoke to my friend on the bus ride here.

Addict: You are the first person who has spoken to me for this long in six months. Other than the good doctor. And those who spoke to me six months ago were the punks who mugged me. They talked at me while kicking me. So, not the best conversation. Do you know what that feels like?

Traveler: No.

Addict: And yet you relegate my state to such a foolish question! (Anger rising) What do *you* know about *me*?

Traveler: (Realizes he is at the wrong and says) I am sorry, I didn't mean to offend you.

Addict: (Smiles slightly and says) You're a good lad.

A few moments pass in silence. Addict is looking at the lights, lost in thought.

Traveler: (Decides to be more perceptive and considerate and says) Didn't you ever have anyone you could talk to?

Addict: I did. But we weren't on the same wavelength. (Looks toward Traveler and recognizes the confusion). The greatest of calamities is when your loved ones don't understand you. You grow distant. You lock yourself up in a little world of your own. (A brief silence, Addict seems to be reminiscing.) Some don't know how to care, others don't even want to. They just dismiss you with "he did it to himself." (Addict turns his head to face Traveler.) Do you think you could ever be weak enough to do something you didn't want to do?

Traveler: No, I don't think so. I don't mean to sound arrogant. I would rather break than bend.

Addict: (With wide eyes to emphasize his message says) When you go home, stranger, bow down to the Greatest for not putting you in a position where you lose yourself. Bow down and thank Him for giving you the chance to live with dignity and not test your patience. For some of us break and lose our way. Bow down and thank Him for not letting you know the miseries of life. (Seeing Traveler does not fully understand, Addict continues) If I cut off one of your toes today, and tomorrow used a cheese grater on the scab for four hours straight every day for a week, how long do you think you would last before losing your will and dignity? (Addict composes himself.) There are things we do not understand. Have the decency and courage to leave room for what you do not know instead of making ... be a little humble. There are things you can't see.

Traveler: (A little dumbfounded, not realizing how naïve he had been but not completely ready to accept what Addict is saying, Traveler questions him.) I don't know what it feels like to be alone nor lonely. But I know people who like being alone. They can spend days at a time.

Addict: You're rattling like the rest. Now think about what you will say before opening your gob. Do you know what it feels like to lose an arm or a leg?

Traveler: But your limbs are just fine.

Addict: (Patience running thin, roars) Didn't I tell you to *think* before talking! You're really dumb for someone so smart! Let's try again. Suppose I had a missing kidney, or a bad heart would you still judge me?

Traveler: (It suddenly dawns upon him.)

Addict: We aren't equal in many ways. One may be strong but not be very good with delicate work. One may be weak but be very strong willed. Similarly pain, whether physical or emotional, may affect one greatly when compared to others. Stop measuring others with the eye of "your" mind. I don't mean there aren't people out there who exaggerate. I am merely asking you not to be quick to judge. See if the person in question actually makes an honest effort to improve their life. Now, please, if you're here to merely confirm your suspicions, then leave me alone. I haven't caused you any harm.

Addict looks like he is weeping, but Traveler can't tell for sure.

Traveler: I am ... sorry.

Addict's expression relaxes and he gives a hearty laugh. Traveler is somewhat getting used to the random episodes of extreme emotion.

Addict: You're a good lad.

Traveler: (With a smile) And you're a patient old man.

Addict laughs and coughs.

Addict: Your friends on the bus let you leave them?

Traveler: They are headed to the village for the fair. I told them I'll catch up. They know me well so they don't impose.

Addict: Ahh. You have youth *and* good friends. I envy you. (Addict has a glazed look.) Tell me what did you hope to learn by talking to me?

Traveler: I'm not sure. (Hesitates thinking it's some kind of a test.)

Addict: Were you hoping for some *profound wisdom?* I am not sure I have any of that. Would you settle for something I wish I knew when I was your age?

Traveler: Yes, please.

Addict: If more is less, and less is more, then perhaps all is nothing, and nothing is all. If not caring can be caring, and caring not caring, then love can be destruction, and destruction can be love. If finding yourself means others find you, then perhaps finding others will lead you to you. If a journey is towards a destination, and your journey is towards you, perhaps then you are the beginning, the journey, and the destination. If you are to reach you, perhaps the latter you is reaching the former you, which means the destination seeks the traveler. Travel. Find yourself, and then become you. If you get lost just remember, you're already at your destination. Stop looking so hard.

Traveler: Wow, I never thought of it like that. That's really deep.

Addict: (Shrugs.)

Some time passed by while they sit in silence.

Traveler: (Feeling more comfortable than before) Didn't your friends or family ever stop you from using?

Addict: They did. But it was already too late by then.

Traveler: Can't you go back?

Addict: Everybody wants to stop the person who is about to kill himself... what's your name boy?

Traveler: Gabriel.

Addict: Gabriel... that's a nice name. See, Gabriel, the thing is when a person is sad and lonely no one really cares to help them. If that person were to stand on a busy bridge and try to talk to people passing by, he would probably be ignored. But if the same person stood on the same bridge with the intention to jump, every other passerby would try to talk him out of it. That is sadly the irony of life. When I sought refuge in drugs, everybody wanted me to stop. But it was too late. I was already on that bridge. It wasn't physical but that's where I stood.

Gabriel is deeply saddened by what Addict said. For in his mind he sees somebody dying slowly right before him, and he is unable to do anything.

Addict: Don't be sad. Learn from it. Look at this beautiful view. Breathe it in, enjoy it. Being sad won't make a difference. Just care for the ones close to you, talk to them. It might help them, and they won't even know it.

Gabriel: (Doesn't lighten up right away but nods. After a few moments of silence Gabriel decides to continue talking.) What's your name?

Addict: (Eyes Gabriel curiously) Hakeem.

Gabriel: Wiseman ... May I ask you something?

Hakeem: (Nods.)

Gabriel: Why are you so lucid? Didn't you just use some when we got off?

Hakeem: (Goes into a laughing fit.) That, my young dumb friend, was medicine. I get off here to enjoy the view and get high. But I haven't actually done that, since I am talking to you.

Gabriel gives Hakeem a quizzical look.

Hakeem: It's some plant that is supposed to help with my cough (and starts laughing.)

Gabriel looks embarrassed and only manages a faint laugh.

Hakeem: The bus will be here shortly. But I'll take the one after.

Saying this Hakeem takes a small piece of paper from his pocket and unfolds it to reveal something that looks like salt. He mixes it with a thick green paste and loads the mixture into a smoking pipe he pulls from his pocket. He lights it. Drag by drag, his face turns into someone without a single worry. As if the glowing flame was personifying his soul: bright, then slowly diminishing. A profound sadness concealed itself in his eyes. Gabriel looks away. Gabriel felt sad. How anyone could let someone go down such a path if all it took was a sincere thought, a short conversation. How could loneliness affect anyone to this extent? Instantly he said a silent prayer and his eyes almost teared up. He thanked God for not knowing what could cause one to become so weak, and for the wisdom to be able to respect how vulnerable humans are.

Hakeem: Oh, you're still here. Tell me something I don't know?

Gabriel: Oh. Uh, I read somewhere that learning new words expands one's mind to new concepts. In other words, one's mind grows. I guess a good example would be the word "decathect." It's when a person withdraws their feelings towards somebody or something, anticipating a future loss.

Hakeem: What a beautiful word. (Hakeem looks lost in thought for a few moments.) It gets too foggy at times, you know. I lose track of reality, or recall memories so often that they barely resemble the facts. But I learned something new today. That's always fun. Makes me feel ... human.

Gabriel: It's not too late you know.

Hakeem: (Doesn't respond, he seems lost, or perhaps focused on something. Gabriel cannot see. Suddenly he starts talking.) Gabriel... you're a good lad. I like you. If I had a son I would have wanted him to be like you. You spoke to me, and you have done everything to save me. Beyond this there is not much you can do.

Gabriel: There must be something.

Hakeem: (To Gabriel's surprise, Hakeem just smiles.) Learn the difference. There are things you cannot change and they will make you kneel if you don't stop trying. (Starts laughing really loud. And then suddenly stops and gives out a wail and cries softly. Looks at Gabriel, then in his tears his face smiled.) I too was a proud man, now I can't even hide my tears.

Gabriel: (Doesn't know what to say. He's never seen a grown man in such a dire state.)

Hakeem: (His eyes locked on the lights) I look at these lights, and I don't feel lonely anymore. It's like when your house isn't empty. You may be doing something by yourself but the fact that your loved ones are close...

Gabriel: (Hears the approach) Hakeem the bus is here. Are you coming?

Hakeem: It's before it's time! (Shakes his head in bitter disapproval.)

Gabriel: Hakeem, are you coming?

Hakeem: (Hears the gentle plea in Gabriel's voice. Takes a deep breath. Gestures his answer by gently shooing Gabriel away.) I'll stay back.

Gabriel barely takes a few steps to where the bus is waiting when he hears his name, in a clear authoritative voice.

Hakeem: (With a stern face) Gabriel. Thank you. (With his expression softening and a goofy smile he says) Good night.

Gabriel: (Seeing this, Gabriel smiles too. Somehow he feels better.) You take care of yourself Hakeem.

Gabriel gets on the bus and takes solace in Hakeem's goofy smile as he waves him away.

Soon Gabriel is with his friends. His closest friend, Slava, tells Gabriel that he cares too much and should relax a little. Gabriel reluctantly accepts the advice, remembering Hakeem's insistence to be happy since there wasn't anything more he could do.

Hours later they take the bus back. The bus reaches where distant lights had danced around like fireflies. There is a small crowd gathered around something, trying to catch a glimpse. An ambulance is present.

People start talking and asking questions of those who have just stepped on the bus. Gabriel and his friends at the back, tired from the fair, were now awake. And what they heard was something like this.

Passengers: What happened? Did someone die? Was that a body?

Passengers: Yes. Some druggy.

Passengers: That's really sad.

Passengers: No, it's not. He brought it onto himself. Some feeble-minded people just give into such a vile thing. I mean, why would you do it if you know it's going to kill you.

Passengers: Did he die of an overdose?

Passengers: Probably. What else could it be?

Gabriel's eyes moisten as the mockery continues. He is too devastated to say anything. Slava sees Gabriel's face and realizes what's happening right away.

Slava: (Stands and slaps the ceiling of the bus really hard. All of his 6 foot 4 inch frame makes the crowd stop and look towards him. When he speaks, his tone is cold enough to send chills down everyone's spine.) By God! If you don't stop disgracing the dead, you will rue this day for the rest of your miserable lives. And if any of you have a doubt, come forth and do not hold me responsible for sending you on your way to hell. (Most passengers avoid his gaze. Some thought to take him on, but something about the young man's calm demeanor told them not to. He sits back down. And asks Gabriel in a soft voice) You okay, buddy? If you want, I'll skin each and every one here.

Gabriel forces a smile and shakes his head, moved by what his friend did for him.

Slava: You knew that guy didn't you? The guy from earlier?

Gabriel: Hakeem. His name was Hakeem. I only spoke to him once.

Slava wanted to tell Gabriel he was being too emotional and caring. But he realized that was one of the reasons they are such close friends.

Gabriel: Hey, Slava.

Slava: Hmm?

Gabriel: I'm really grateful to have a friend like you. Thought you should know that.

Slava: (Not fully sure where Gabriel is coming from, puts his hand behind Gabriel's shoulder and holds it firmly.) Bossman, it goes without saying. You're like a brother to me. (After a little hesitation) Now tell me, are you okay?

Gabriel: (Takes a deep breath and manages a smile that he actually means.) Yes.

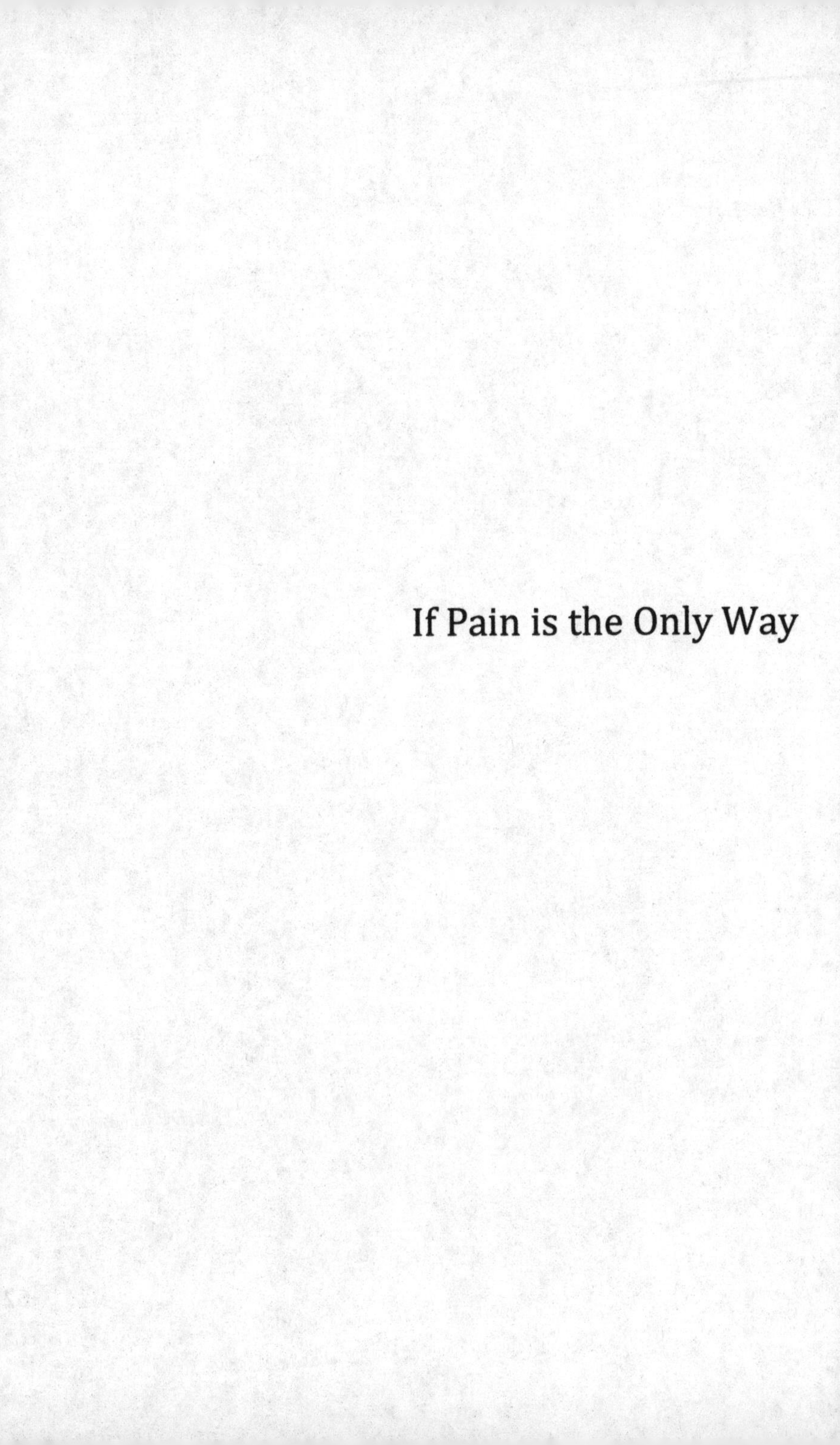

If Pain is the Only Way

If Pain is the Only Way

On a journey with no destiny

My quest ends by starting the next

My eyes only know how to seek

Do not take away my sight by showing me what I wish to see

I move without moving

The world passes me by

I exist only to bear my shackles

Do not take away my freedom by setting me free

Tireless days and cold, starry nights

I live today, for tomorrow I may not be

My loyalty is only to the moment in which I live

Do not take my sanctuary away by sancturaizing me

Let me smile

Let me dream of heaven with eyes open

Let me enjoy this slumber of ignorance

Let me be happy and live my destined life

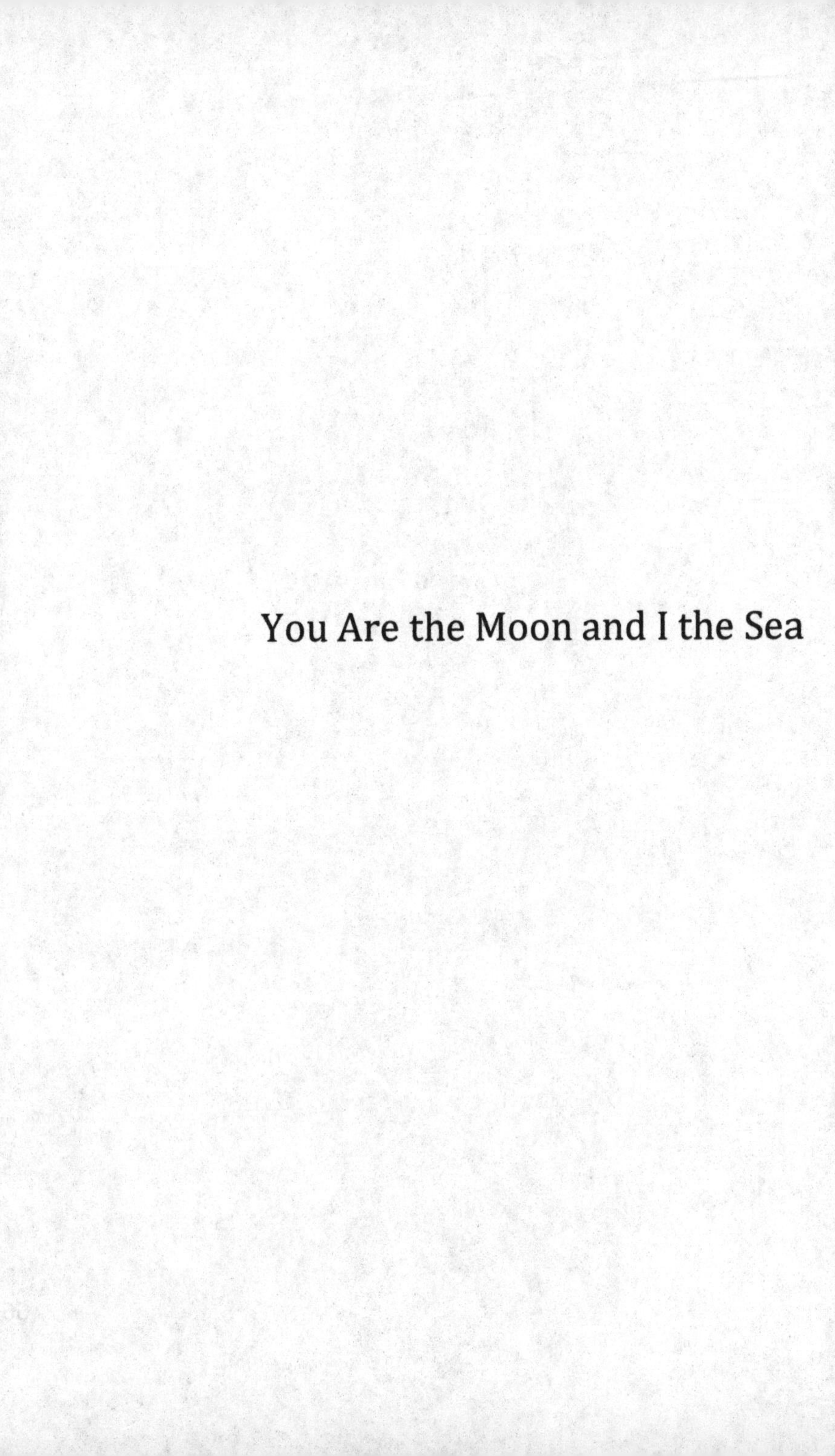

You Are the Moon and I the Sea

I am dark, lifeless, within myself alive. Those who approach me dread me, fear me. The sheer intensity of my darkness sparks fear into the very souls of those who can see. They shudder, shiver, and look away.

My spirits are lifted when you are close by. As I bask in your light, my surroundings illuminated with your love. Not only I but even those around me feel it, understand it, and cherish it. How euphoric is your presence that the love you bring me even others relish. Those who fear my cruelty, the travelers who dread getting lost within me, they celebrate and sing songs of happiness when they see the way I change in your presence.

The look on your face bewitches me; I smile to you, for you. Along with those who are insane to many, I care not what the world may think. I break the chains of what is expected from my character and dance to your rhythm and harmony. Loud waves and sands limned in silver brag and confess my love for you.

And when it is time for you to leave. I settle down. My pain exudes from the very smile that you brought with you. Without you I become lifeless again. Turbulent and violent as I may be, nothing moves me like you do. No words can pacify me the way your silence does. No one can hold me the way you do.

Such is our love and our curse. I shall see you and seek you until eternity. Look at you from afar, riddle myself by your looks, but never be with you. Know this my beloved, I have happily chosen your love over any earthly happiness or being. I regret not and shall wait for you as ever, to come and shine over me, enchant me.

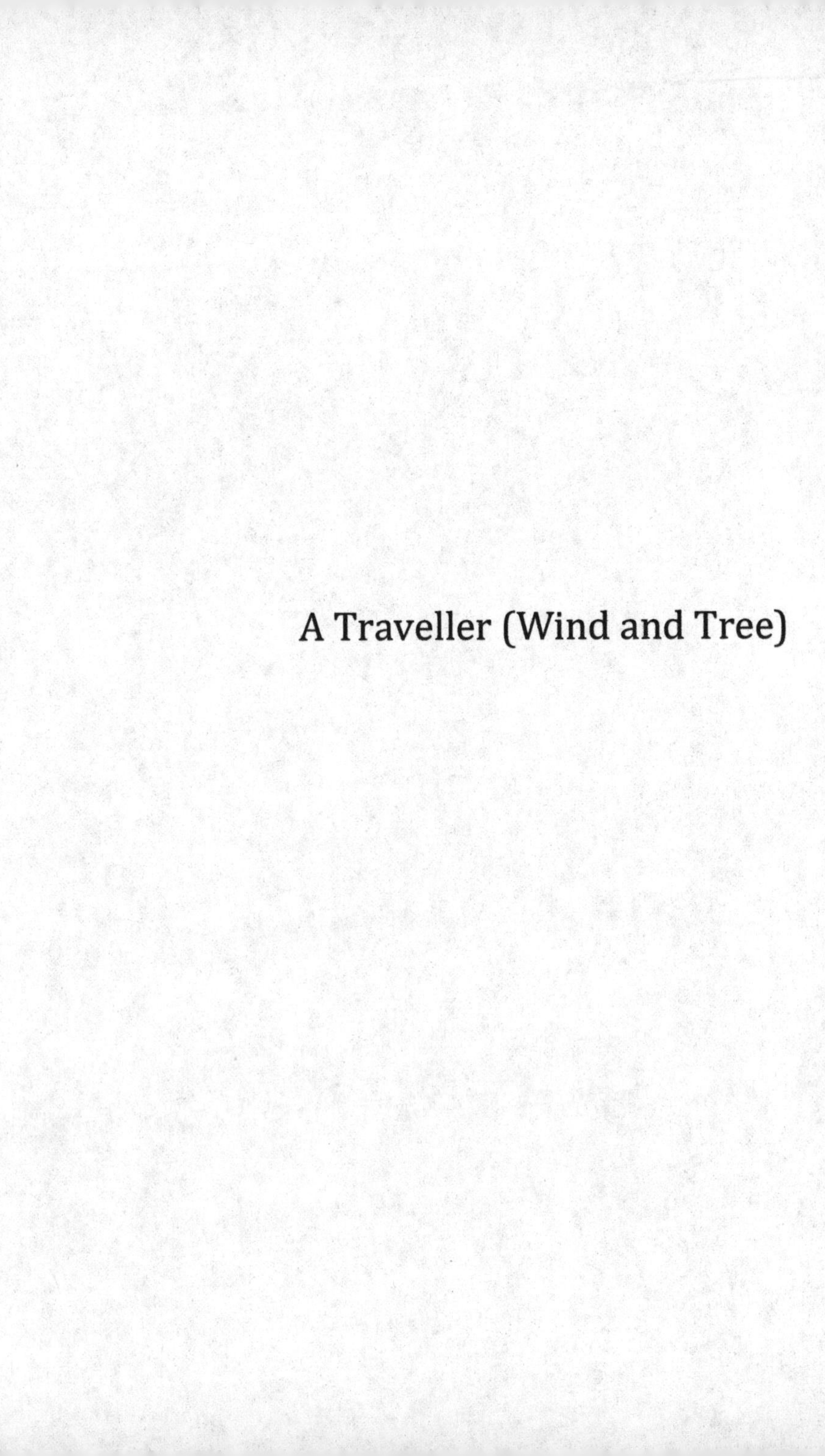

A Traveller (Wind and Tree)

A Traveller (Wind and Tree)

A traveller (Wind) sets pillow and spreads out on grass. Under the dark night's sky, Wind breathes heavily. Wind mentally collects all the necessaries for tomorrow's journey, and once satisfied Wind starts to drift. Remembering an equally beautiful night, Wind smiles, drifting further into that familiar world. Reliving the moments.

Some odd moons ago—what felt, in Wind's mind, like an eternity, yet somehow not long enough—Wind swept through a village, where he met Tree. Intelligence and strength made Tree stand out. Wind noticed how Tree spoke but never really said anything, smiled and laughed but seemed detached from the moment.

Wind spoke to Tree a few times. As much intrigued as Wind was, Wind chose to keep away. Wind would speak to Tree now and then. They were somewhat friends but not close. Wind realized Tree, in general, was a cynic. Wind wondered if it was wind's place to ponder about it, to think about Tree.

Wind was set to leave the following morning. Wind, out of habit, went out one last time to capture in memory the place that served as a temporary sanctuary. Wind noticed Tree standing alone in the silence. Tree's expression was ever so peaceful and subtle, but inwardly troubled and restless. Wind decided to talk to Tree.

Wind approached, making enough noise to let Tree recover from the mood Tree was radiating. So that Tree did not lose face.

Wind: Pleasant night, is it not?

Tree: (Without looking) Indeed it is. (Turned gaze towards wind.) How are you wind?

Wind: I am well, and all set for tomorrow. How are you, Tree?

Tree: I am good. I hear you are leaving tomorrow? (Wind noticed Tree was not fully there but remained quiet.)

Wind: Yes I am. All set for it. Came out for a stroll, out of habit, and I saw you standing here. (Wind looked towards the crowd, hustling and bustling, while talking to Tree) You … (he waited for Tree to follow Wind's own gaze) do not like mixing? (Tree smiled.) (Wind quickly added) I hope you don't mind my asking.

Tree: I do, just not tonight. I felt like staying on my own for a while.

Wind: Hmm I see. I shall leave you to it then.

Wind began to make a move.

Tree: It's fine.

They stayed in silence for a good few seconds. Wind breathed in the scenery: the stream with its little rippling, the stars shimmering in the distance, and the ambient noises from the crowd. All of this changed Wind's mood. Wind decided to talk to Tree at a deeper level and see if Wind could be of any help.

Wind: It's beautiful. Is it not?

Tree: (Almost immediately) Yes, it is.

Wind: Then why the gloominess?

Tree: (Surprised at getting caught, Tree tried to recover) Who said I was gloomy?

Wind: (Smiled in a peculiar way, Tree recognized it but did not know what it meant. Wind looked at Tree from the corner of the eye in a harmless manner.) Am I being inappropriate?

Tree: No. but I'm not sad. (Tree hoped the bluff didn't get called. At the same time wondered, hoped that someone actually understood.)

Wind: When you gaze into the distance your eyes seem as if they do not see what is before them.

Tree: Are you trying to make sense out of something that doesn't require making sense of?

Wind: (Smiled again out of habit, paused, and decided to change approach) Are you a cynic, Tree?

Tree: I am not sure how to answer that. I am me.

Wind: Do you doubt what you see?

Tree: I do not doubt nor disbelieve what I know. (Again deflected the question.)

Wind: (Enjoyed the chase and closing of the trap) So in other words, you do not disbelieve feelings, you merely do not know what to believe in. Am I close?

Tree: (Tree rustled a bit in evaluating the statement.) Yes, you are close. However, I am a believer.

Wind: I never doubted nor questioned that for a second. (Turned to face tree. Wondered if the solution wind had in mind is a solution or a sheer act of selfishness. Wind decided to go with it.) Do you believe in love, Tree?

Tree: No.

Wind: Why not?

Tree: What was once loved can be hated. What is love if it comes and goes? What causes one to love and then stop? How can one believe or disbelieve a feeling so unreliable?

Wind: (Smiled out of sheer happiness.) I ... do not know how to answer all those questions. One can argue this and that to no avail. (Faced Tree with a lot of movement in order to disconnect them from the topic at hand.) May I ask a favor of you?

Tree: (Taken aback by the sudden change in mood.) Mmm. Please do.

Wind: (Very excited, and with a grave demeanor.) I am leaving tomorrow, and I do not see how this may bring about any harm. You may dislike me for it one day ... but then again, I may be getting ahead of myself. I tell you all this... (seeing the perplexed look on tree's face wind stopped and exhaled deeply). Would you let me— allow me—to fall in love with you?

Tree: (Flabbergasted) *How*?

Wind: Well, you don't have to do anything. Just give me eleven minutes. To be yours and to have you: to be free to think of you, and to worry about you if need be.

Tree: (Incredulously) Eleven minutes?

Wind: Yes, it is not long. Everything will be as it was. Only that a fool will be happier after that time span.

Tree: (Tree couldn't fathom the reasoning behind this. But there was something about the way Wind was looking at Tree. Wind did not seem desperate nor pitiful, but there was something about it that Tree hadn't seen before… vulnerability, hope, happiness, excitement, life maybe even all of these.) I do not know what you will achieve from these "eleven minutes". However, I am at your disposal.

Wind: Ahhh. How you've made me happy. (Without waiting for tree to understand, Wind advanced firmly towards Tree) in this moment I am yours and you are mine. In this moment I can close my eyes and still be happy for I can think of you without guilt. My heart beats harder … for you. In this moment nothing exists beyond you and whatever exists beyond you is not without you, for you are in my heart and mind. In this moment I am truly happy because of you. I love you.

Tree: (Laughed without mirth but in amusement) You sound like you've gone mad. (Tried to resist what Wind was radiating, for Tree was not familiar with it. Hence, cautious and a little fearful.)

Wind: (Smiled and looked at Tree in a way that captivated Tree in warmth.) Does it matter? I am happy.

Tree: (Tree realized it and was happy for Wind, not fully understanding why.) So, what next?

Wind: (As if responding yet ignoring Tree's question) You have breathed in a little of me. I'll always be with you, a part of you. Not to exist but merely to be. You don't understand?

Tree: (A little embarrassed) No.

Wind: Close your eyes. Now, do you need to see me to know I am here?

Tree: I know you're here because I can hear you.

Wind: In that case ….

After a few moments.

Tree: Well…!

Moments later

Tree: What's wrong?

(Tree realized Wind was looking straight at Tree with a gentle smile. Tree felt shy.)

Tree: Why didn't you say anything?

Wind: When you don't need to see me to know I'm with you, then I shall just… be.

(Tree didn't fully understand, how anyone could "just be.")

Silence.

Tree: Why eleven minutes?

Wind: With you, every moment is an eternity, and all of eternity just a moment. (A faint smile crossed Wind's face that was almost not there). Besides, it shouldn't make a difference, at least not to you. We've got four minutes left.

Tree: You're keeping count?

Wind: For your sake, yes.

(Tree looked at Wind, Wind leaned back with eyes shut and in a moment started smiling.)

Tree: Why are you smiling?

Wind: Because you're looking at me.

Tree: (A little embarrassed for being caught) So?

Wind: Nothing really. It just makes me happy, makes me smile.

Wind gazed into the distance. It wasn't a full moon that night but everything that met the eye was bathed in silver light. It was quiet to the point where even smiles could be heard and calm enough for gazes to be felt.

Wind: It's beautiful. Just, beautiful.

Tree: You like the moon, don't you?

Wind: (Without looking at Tree) Yes. But what makes all of this special is being in the company of someone who is special.

Tree followed Wind's gaze and for the first time in years noticed the beauty that surrounded them. There was something fairly peculiar about it. Tree wondered why it was different. Tree had seen this view for as long as Tree existed, and had certainly seen more beautiful nights.

The moon wasn't perfect but certainly shed light everywhere. The stars were one big family that took away the emptiness of the sky. The stream made a noise that marred the silence but never the peace. Everything was far away yet felt so close, distinct but interconnected.

Perhaps it was because of Wind, the scents and beautiful night noises that Wind carried or maybe it was Wind's companionship. Maybe Tree saw everything through Wind's eyes…

Tree's thoughts were interrupted.

Wind started talking, but Wind's tone was different.

Wind: Well that's that.

Tree: What do you mean?

Wind: Times up.

Tree: Oh.

Wind: Thank you very much. It meant a lot to me.

Tree: It's really nothing. I don't understand what you could have gained. (Tree appeared composed on the surface, but that wasn't the case on the inside.)

Wind: I am a traveler. I have no home, no one to ask me of what I feel—or if I feel at all. My home is my memories, and thanks to you now I have a warm corner where I can sit and revisit this night.

Tree: But I don't love you. You were just dreaming.

Wind: I carry your scent, and you have breathed in some of me.

Whether you like it or not I am taking a part of you with me and leaving a part of me here. That is love enough for me. As for dreaming, do we all not dream? Do we not try and hope for a beautiful dream to recur? The only difference is, I can.

Tree: You sound different?

Wind: (Smiled pleasantly but somehow distant) That is because you are not mine to think of anymore.

(Tree felt as if something were amiss. Not good or bad just not there.)

Tree smiled.

Tree: I enjoyed our conversation very much. It was refreshing.

Wind: (Smiled heartily) I have to go now. I have to leave early in the morning tomorrow.

Tree: (Tree nodded) Hmm.

Wind: Take care, Tree. And be well.

Tree: Have a safe journey. Goodbye.

The following morning Tree was doing daily chores. Wind stood on a hill and briefly looked back. It looked beautiful—then again, everything did in the early hours. At the very same moment Tree gazed towards the hills and wondered if Wind would ever think about Tree. A moment later both went about their day.

Wind returns from the solace of memories and wonders if it really happened. How Tree is doing? If Wind should continue to think about Tree? Finally, like always, Wind decides to smile about it and goes to sleep.

Sparkling Eyes

He thinks that the sound of my laughter soothes him. As if my presence makes everything beautiful. He speaks as if he could spend an eternity holding my gaze. He says that stars shimmer in the little tears that form in my eyes and accentuate every moment with their sparkling. I asked him if my tears make him happy and he said, "May God forbid sadness from coming close to you."

He looks at me in ways I cannot describe. Sometimes I just can't tell what he is thinking. In one moment he is with me and the next he is gone. His smile is as secretive as his eyes, which never give anything away. How then do I believe what he says? Does he really believe what he says, or is he too naïve to know that he is deceiving himself? Does he not see: I am a mere human and my smile… ordinary?

She doubts my words; or perhaps it is my spirit that lacks. I cannot tell her what she is, for I fear scaring her away. So fragile I see her that even a whisper may cause her to fade. She chooses to be who she is and I … I judge her not, but continue to love her. I see her hiding at times behind smiles and words. I let her, believing tonight is not the night I learn of the pain that resides in her. But when she smiles, only she remains. I feel as if life itself has become beautiful. As pure as the warmth of sunlight, as honest as a child's prayer, and as close to me as my very heartbeat.

Does she not realize that I see her looking at me, stealing glances here and there? I wonder what she thinks of me. Is it so hard for her to believe that when she laughs time stands still for me? Naïve I may be, even unwise, but what difference does that make? Does she not understand that, to me, she is not a mere human and her smile nothing earthly?

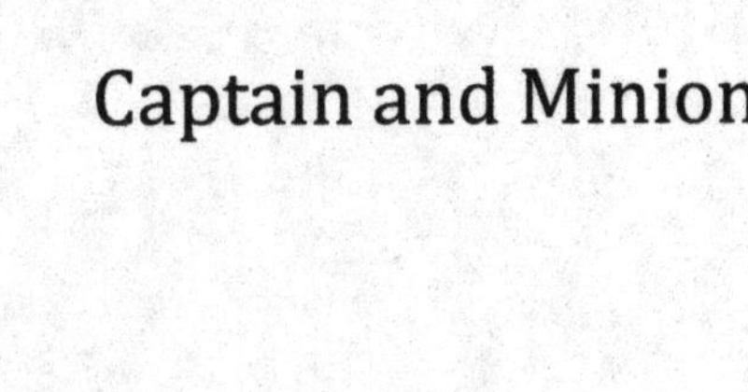

Captain and Minion

Captain is a man of many colours, a wandering soldier who roams the city of Karaksh and its outskirts. He doesn't necessarily travel in search of knowledge—at least, not anymore. Captain happens to be one of the best swordsmen in the country.

"Minion" is merely 14. As an orphan he was overwhelmed with the vicissitudes that life presented him. Then he met Captain.

It is hard to say what they are to each other, father and son, brothers, or friends, perhaps all of the above. They lead a very modest lifestyle. Usually sleeping at military camps, check posts, or, weather permitting, they sleep in their sleeping bags. They carried nothing other than their swords, sleeping bags, a spare set of clothes, and some provisions.

Minion has been lead to believe that Captain is a messenger, who oversees the needs of camps. He doesn't report to anyone. He usually finds a letter, at a camp, that has instructions and writes a letter back of his findings. People respect him but he is not necessarily seen as a figure of authority.

Minion has never seen Captain arguing, or losing his temper. Except when they first met. This was some odd moons ago when Minion was a mere child of 7. Minion was sitting next to a high-end tea shop. The vendor had already told Minion to leave once. Minion shied away, but hunger kept him within view. The vendor returned to him with harsh words. Minion took his time. Partly hoping to convince the vendor otherwise. The shop owner shoved him and shouted at him. Being famished and weak Minion fell down and started to get up. With dignity and hope draining out of the child, who barely understood what dignity and hope meant. Minion stood up slower than the vendor's patience allowed. In one swift motion, the vendor brought his cane down on the child's back, striking him again and again. Surprisingly, the waif did not move, nor even hold up an arm in defense: he simply squatted there, sobbing silently. At this point Captain who witnessed the whole thing approached the well-dressed man and asked him politely to stop, and said that he was just a hungry child. The vendor eyed Captain, taking in his humble garb. The vendor was repulsed by what he saw. He barked some insults and said that it was bad for business to have a filthy, lazy child hanging around his shop front. The vendor said that the child needed to learn a lesson and continued thrashing. The thumping of the cane meeting the child's back was the only sound, everybody who saw this walked along silently with their gaze averted. Before the vendor could strike again, Captain swiftly seized the vendor's arm and asked him calmly, "Do you have any children?" To which the vendor angrily tried to push Captain out of the way shouting obscenities and threats. Captain effortlessly, held the seized arm high and kicked the vendor's foot out, bringing him to the ground. He waited for the vendor to realise what was happening, and then punched him in the gut so hard the tea vendor forgot how to breathe. Captain repeated the question.

Captain: Do you have any children?

Vendor: (Writhing with pain) yes, why?

Captain: Thank them. For I spare your life for their sake. (And with this Captain brought down his sword, still in its scabbard, on the vendor's ribs. Captain estimated three broken ribs, he was right.) (In a voice that would make stones seek refuge) Let this be your lesson.

Soldiers approached the scene. The vendor who was cowering and trying to fathom what had happened gained some confidence and yelled at the soldiers to arrest the man. The soldiers look at Captain's expression and hesitated. Captain showed them something and said something to them that made them perspire profusely. Captain picked up Minion, still cowering, in his arms and took him away. They never spoke about that day. Minion never asked, and Captain never answered.

In the years that follow, Captain trained Minion like a father. Combat arts, writing, and philosophy were just a few of the subjects. Captain made sure Minion trained with other soldiers whenever possible. They shared workloads like brothers, and, in their leisure time, they acted like friends: so much so, that it was hard to tell who the elder was.

Minion is now fourteen. Their latest job kept them at a camp for two months to help in the building of a new barracks. However, a day before their departure, upon Minion's request, they went to a fair that was in town. They walked around and ate what they could afford. The storytellers started singing, and a small crowd started to gather. Minion wanted to go and listen to the story, and, after much persistence, Captain finally relents.

The tale was about a young man who falls in love with a young girl. Circumstances wouldn't let them meet. So, they decided to die together. Of course, the story was told at length with feigned sadness and tears. Captain loudly fakes a few tears and blows his nose, Minion didn't pay attention since he was lost in his own thoughts. Captain threw his arm over Minion, which got some attention from the storytellers. Who were now collecting in bags and hats what the audience was willing to spare.

Captain: You, sir, are brilliant. How do you bring so much ... out of telling a tale?

Storyteller: (Smiled a much practiced smile) Such is the power of love–I am but a simple human being. What could I possibly bring? Let your generosity reflect your appreciation.

Captain: (Fishing his pockets and playing his part too well) You're worth your weight in gold. Sadly, I have forgotten my coin purse at home.

Storyteller: (Another fake smile) Of course, sir.

Captain: But I am sure my friend here will not disappoint you.

Minion knew he would have to pay for his insistence to come to the play, but he didn't know it would be in money. Minion felt the storyteller's gaze on him like a dead weight. He glares up at Captain, but gives what he can.

Captain: Is that (points to a food stall) one of yours?

Storyteller: Yes, sir.

Captain: Then we shall show our support. Come Minion, let's buy something.

Minion felt the storyteller's gaze again and nudges Captain. Captain ignores Minion and announces he wants a baked potato. Minion feels defeated and Captain victorious. They both leave.

Minion: (Glaring at captain) You have your coin purse!

Captain just grins while eating.

Minion: You made me pay. Twice!

Captain: You made me go there and listen. (Acting all serious) You know how I get hungry when I hear emotionally touching stories. I start to perspire profusely and feel weak—

Minion: You're a glutton. You eat all the time. You just don't get fat! And you're a miser.

Captain: (Gasps in horror.) Didn't I buy you rice cakes the other day?

Minion: That was three months ago! And you've mentioned it like a hundred times.

Captain: Three months? Are you sure?

Minion steps on Captain's shoe, throwing him off balance. He swiftly takes the baked potato out of Captain's hand.

Captain: I let you take it. It's not good; you'll get a stomach ache.

Minion eats without a word. Captain wonders how long before he won't be able to read Minion's attacks. By the looks of it, it wouldn't be long. Captain felt proud of Minion, but no words were said.

They start their journey the next morning leaving without much ceremony. For a good few miles Minion stayed quiet. Captain knew what Minion was thinking about, and he gave Minion space. Minion was taught by Captain to think. Think about everything and nothing, so that Minion himself would answer questions he was capable of. However, leaving room for the possibility of being wrong. Finally, Minion concluded that he did not know enough, and spoke to Captain.

Minion: Captain?

Captain: Hmm?

Minion: What is love?

Captain: Is that what you have been thinking about?

Minion: Yes.

Captain: What do you think it is?

Minion: I'm not sure. The storyteller said "Wind" and "Tree" loved each other wholeheartedly and selflessly, and they both died for each other: an example of true love. Does that mean love is dying for someone? If that's the case, was it not true love before their deaths?

Captain: (With a smile) My days, Minion. You're asking the right questions. It is a matter of perspective. The basic idea would be caring for someone very much. Liking them to the point that just thinking about them is a reason to smile. You want them to be happy. In my experience—which, quite frankly, is limited—love is an emotion, like happiness, sadness, or fear. Like fear, love can be strong or weak, obscure or apparent. At times we ourselves don't know what we fear until we have to confront it. (Leaves it there so that Minion can digest it.)

Minion: (After a short pause) And how is dying relevant?

Captain: It was in the story because it laced the love story with grief and sadness. Many people don't like plain wise stories. They like drama and grief. As for real life, death does happen, but it doesn't necessarily show love. It could be weakness, selfishness, and so on. Imagine if "Tree" had moved on as "Wind" had suggested. Perhaps they would have found happiness. When things don't work out, you leave your beloved so they may find happiness elsewhere. You don't want them to die.

Minion: Not even for yourself, Captain?

Captain: Heavens no! Especially not for yourself.

Minion: Didn't the storyteller say, "Once you truly love you can never forget—such is the power of love?"

Captain: For the sake of the argument I'll pretend you didn't believe every single word he uttered. Remember your fear of horses? Why did you fear them?

Minion: You know why.

Captain: Humour me.

Minion: When I was a kid a horse almost bit my hand off.

Captain: And now you ride them. Why do you think that is? What happened to the fear?

Minion: You told me that tame horses don't bite. (With a slight plaintive tone) You lied, though, they do bite at times. But you used that to teach me how to ride. I was scared at first, but eventually I got over it. The fear was all in my head I guess.

Captain: You like horses now, right?

Minion: Yes, I do.

Captain: Same principle applies here. You said it yourself: "it was all in my head." At times you love someone and then you realise it was all in your head. In reality, they aren't who you thought they were. You were blinded by your emotion, so blinded that at times you love bad people. (Captain seems slightly distant. Minion, from experience, can tell, others would not have been able to.)

Minion: If you love someone and they knew it, wouldn't it make things work? Like, wouldn't it convince the other person to be a better person?

Captain: What happened with Jacob? (Captain is referring to a general's son who was visiting a camp. Minion and Jacob became friends). You befriended him against my wishes, and then stopped being his friend. Why?

Minion: We were friends until he called me a lowly servant boy. He didn't say it as a joke.

Captain: What does that have to do with your friendship? Didn't you care for him as a friend? Didn't he know that?

Minion: I cared a lot and he knew it! You don't belittle your friend or comrade.

Captain: Exactly. Sometimes, love isn't enough. Things just don't work out. Would you have befriended him if you'd known about his character beforehand?

Minion: No.

Captain: Do you think you could have seen his nature had you not befriended him and avoided it?

Minion: Yes.

Captain: But you wanted a friend so much that you didn't stop to see.

Minion: (Looks gloomy.)

Captain: Chin up boy. Be happy you learned a lesson and didn't have to go through any suffering. What if he humiliated you in front of people by calling you a servant boy in their presence?

Minion: (Considers this and is glad that it didn't happen. Ready to change the topic for now and burning with curiosity) Captain, have you ever been in love?

Captain: (As if waiting for the inevitable) You're five years too young to ask me that question.

Minion: Yes, Captain.

They walk in silence for a while

Minion: Captain, what is the power of love?

Captain: Oh ... It is something beyond words. It could bring life to barren lands. (Minion seems interested.) Keep you warm on freezing nights. (Minion is wide eyed.) It can move mountains. Make the cruelest of rulers melt.

Minion: (Asks excitedly) Really!

Captain: No. (Grins.)

Minion: (Neither happy nor amused.)

Captain: It's you and solely you. You may reduce a mountain to rubble so you could see your beloved's house before you go to sleep. It's how much you want it and how stupid you will be about

it. People say it's the power of love and what not, it's all just...
stories.

The road they tread has open fields on both sides. Refugees from a
war torn country are camping, scattered like leaves from a
withered tree. Minion slows down a little when he sees them.

Minion: Isn't there anything we could do about them?

Captain: (Who by now is looking straight ahead) Which ones?
There are so many.

Minion looks at the people who return the gaze. Some of the
nomads look at Minion and Captain with curiosity, others with
contempt. The children point and whisper to one another. One
child slightly older than the others, wearing tattered clothes starts
walking beside Minion, a stick on his side that he grips like a sword.
The other kids start giggling. Someone shouts something at the kid
who quickly runs to the field. The same man yells at the kids, and
they scatter.

Some refugees have livestock and seem in better health than
others, but most are in bad shape. The hidden desperation and
silent cries begin to bother minion. He looks at captain. Captain is
walking with an iron-like expression. This daunts Minion from
saying anything.

Along the road there are some richly-clad locals, mostly on horses.
Some of the refugees follow them persistently. At first the rich

ignore them but quickly turn to harsh words and low remarks. At this, two out of three of the refugees turn away. The one still walking along is a young woman with a small child, her health and clothes in bad shape. She asks every man and woman in the group. Some of the rich cover their nose and push her away. Someone says, "Why don't you go back to your own country and beg there? This is our country! We don't want beggars here." Some of them show their agreements with a loud "yes". One seemingly richer man on his horse made no eye contact with her. Desperate, she pulls at his leg. The mother falls, and her baby cries loudly. She tries to placate him not looking away from her baby. She curses herself, her baby, and life in general. She wondered if she should kill herself and her child. The rich man wasn't satisfied and saw Captain and Minion coming. He got off his horse.

Merchant: Soldier, did you see that? This woman has been constantly harassing us. I demand you teach this barbaric low life a lesson. Let them know, we, in this country, are honourable people. We do not condone begging. Lock her up. Filthy woman!

Captain: (Expressionless) Do you have any children, sir?

Merchant: (Surprised by the question and points at the civilian) Yes. I don't see how that is relevant. I said arrest her!

Captain: (Draws his sword. At which a lot of gasps are heard.) Are you hurt ma'am?

The woman, wild eyed, rocks her child and covers his face with her free hand as if shielding him from Captain.

Merchant: Are you out of your mind? Just arrest her.

Captain: (With his free hand, Captain grabs the merchant's collar and shakes him. Some of the local women give out a little scream. If any of your "honourable men" come any closer I will not show mercy. Minion! Make sure I am not interrupted. (Captain draws his sword with his free hand.)

Some of the rich leave hurriedly. Minion, an obedient soldier, stands with his back to Captain and the merchant, his sword drawn to the crowd.

Captain: (Looks at the woman) I apologise on behalf of my countrymen.

Merchant: What is the meaning of this? Are you—

Captain: (Presses his sword against the merchant's chest.)

Captain: Ma'am how would you like me to punish this man? Please bear in mind he has children.

Woman: There's no need. I am fine. It was my mistake. I shouldn't have bothered anyone.

Captain: (Looks Merchant dead in the eye.) You see, sir, when this honourable woman had unbridled power she forgave you, and when you were stronger you chose to kick a helpless mother. Some of your "honourable" friends left you, while the rest stood by and watched. And you dare speak of honour! Leave. (Releases the merchant.) Minion, let them go.

Minion does as told. The group speaks to each other in hushed voices, some swearing to get back at Captain for this. Captain ignores them. Captain and Minion sheath their swords, and their grave expression soften.

Captain: (Reaches for his small pouch of money. He hands it to the young mother.)

Woman: Thank you. Oh, thank you sir. God will reward you a hundred times over.

Captain: Why don't you find a job? Or do you dislike work?

Woman: I tried, sir. I couldn't find anything. Most people chase us away just because our skin is lighter.

Captain asks Minion for a piece of paper and quickly writes on it. He folds it and fishes about in his pockets, pulling out a small handkerchief. He hands both to the young mother. Minion's eyes widen as he recognizes the insignia on the handkerchief.

Captain: Take those in dire need with you to the military camp in the town and give this to the head of the camp. Show the handkerchief to the guards first. They will find you jobs. You shall never have to beg again. Please take care of your child.

The lady started praising him and called him an angel. Captain barely smiled, but he looked at the child, and smiled at the child who was quiet now.

With that, Captain quickly walks away, Minion right behind him. He looks at some of the others coming to the woman. She talks to them, and they start smiling with their eyes seeming to shine with hope, or perhaps Minion wanted to remember it like that.

Minion: We did a good thing didn't we? They look happy.

Captain: Helping others is good.

Minion: (After some silence.) I saw that, you know.

Captain: Uh huh.

Minion: You're the "wandering demon"!

Captain: I doubt it.

Minion: The emperor's youngest yet most valuable retainer. The wandering demon who keeps all the forces in line. You're a legend.

Captain: You shouldn't believe all the stories you hear.

Minion: But you are! How come you never told me?

Captain: It never came up. What difference does it make?

Minion: Uh … not much, I guess. You're still the same person. Just richer, and much more … legendary.

Captain: (A little exhausted) What did I tell you about stories?

Minion: What was it like, tell me?

Captain: (Looks at Minion's pleading eyes, and thinks. After a brief pause he starts laughing loudly, a joyous rumble.)

Minion: (Used to such reaction) Captain.

Captain: We shall come back to that question later. All in good time.

Minion: Captain, please.

Captain: All in good time.

Minion: (Doesn't press anymore.)

Silence. Minion is still thinking about the incident that happened. He's fought off bigger men. Stabbed them too. But never to help anyone. He keeps thinking about the young child in the mother's arms.

Captain: Minion.

Minion: Hmm.

Captain: If I ever see you reduce a mountain to rubble for your beloved while there are people like the ones we just saw, I'll kill you.

Minion: (Knew that the captain meant it.) Yes, Captain.

Captain: Make her happy. Just don't live in a bubble that blinds you from seeing what's right in front of you.

Minion: Yes, Captain.

Captain: You have to love people you know. You just have to. This is love too. Do you understand?

Minion: Captain, wouldn't that be compassion?

Captain: (Eyes Minion, a part of him feels a pang of sorrow for Minion. A mere child who had to grow up before his age. He vows to give Minion some good childhood memories. Captain smacks the back of Minion's head who is not expecting it.) You are right... But you sounded cheeky! Besides your guard was down. You deserve another one. (Minion dodges it.) What is love without compassion... a mere obsession.

Minion: (Takes the lesson, and punches Captain's side.) You let your guard down.

Captain: (Stops walking) Why you dirty little devil.

Minion runs, and Captain chases him. They exchange blows and wrestle lightly, laughing all the way. Minion jumps on Captain's back, who lets him be for a few minutes.

Captain: You're getting fat, boy. How about you carry me?

Minion: (Gets off.) No, thank you.

At the next town, they stop at a tea house for refreshments. It is a much-needed break for both of them.

Minion: Captain, what is falling in love like?

Captain: You know when you're really sleepy and are trying to stay awake. You rest your head and next thing you know some sound wakes you up. Only then do you realise you were asleep. It's just as natural and just as difficult not to.

Minion: (Thinks but doesn't really think. Hesitates a little) And... What's it like to be in love?

Captain: (Pretends he doesn't notice.) It is a beautiful feeling. You feel like you're in a dream. In this case too, like fear, imagination is your worst enemy. You start thinking about things that don't exist. Sadly, you start believing them too. You don't think about consequences, you just want them to be with you and be happy.

Minion: Like Azazel? (Refers to a wolf Minion tried to tame and keep as a pet.)

Captain: Spot on. So the right thing to do would be to look for logical outcomes. Compatibility, goals in life, and so on.

Minion: (Is quiet but seems troubled... Captain waits a little.)

Captain: Out with it, boy. Say it. (Not loud but commanding.)

Minion: What about parents' love, Captain? Do you think my parents loved me?

Captain: Of course they did. Almost all parents love their children. Only the unfortunate ones don't. Listen carefully, I'll only say this once: you would make any father proud and any mother happy.

Minion: (Sulks. Moist eyes.) Captain, I wish I had parents. I think about them. If I were with them I would never love anyone else over them.

Captain: (Lets Minion have his say. He listens intently.)

Minion: (Deep in thought) And I know I am young and whatnot, but I am really grateful you took care of me. It means the world to me. (His voice breaks, and Minion begins to sob like the little boy he is.)

Captain: (Captain holds Minion by his shoulders and says in a soft voice) Minayil, look at me. (Minion does not comply. Captain lets go of one shoulder and reaches for Minion's chin and lifts it so Minion faces him. Minion looks up.) I may not be your real father, but, believe me, I have always seen you as my son, and nothing will change that. If I get married and have children they will be your siblings and their mother, your mother. In my absence you will take care of them. You will, won't you? (Minion nods and starts crying uncontrollably. Captain embraces him and kisses his head. He lets him cry for a few minutes.) Okay, that's enough. (Pushes him away lightly.) Wipe your tears. (Smiles at him.) Let's go, and wipe your snot, soldier. You look like a little bunny with a wet nose.

Minion cracks a half-hearted smile. They start walking and Minion wipes his face and gains his composure but not completely.

Captain: Fix yourself. You don't want to be called a crybaby at the palace, do you?

Minion: (Jerks his head up) The palace!

Captain: (Smiles) Would you like to go there?

Minion: Can we, really? (With a little cynicism) You're not joking, or are you?

Captain: No joke. That's where we are headed right now. That's why I was laughing earlier. I wanted to explain to you about loyalty and commitment. I didn't know where to start. And you started talking about (makes an annoying face) "the power of love". (Minion is too happy to react to Captain's taunts.) I found the timing amusing. Just remember this: let your loyalty and commitment show your love, not your words. Do you understand?

Minion: Yes, sir. Captain, when we get there, can I have my own bed? (At the camps Minion would have to sleep in the barracks with smelly and untidy beds.)

Captain: Of course, my son.

Minion: (Minion practically skips along beside Captain. Suddenly, he slows.) Captain, what if they don't let me in?

Captain: (Smiles, but it's not a simple smile: there is something dark about it, aggressive, and slightly demonic.) Oh, they will. (Minion had never seen this before. Perhaps it was a father being protective of his child, or a glimpse of the captain who had lead battalions to raging wars, perhaps both. Either way it made Minion feel secure.)

Minion beams like the sun. He doesn't have a single care in the world. He smiles and walks next to his father enjoying being a son.